There's Only One YOU

For Bennett and Nora . . . each delightfully *unique!*
LOVE FROM GRANDMA KATIE

For Kyla Ecle . . . *uniquely* beautiful!
LOVE FROM AUNTIE DEBBIE

To Lee Lee and Penny Marie, and also to Cherie, Michelle,
and their *beautiful* baby, with lots of love.
—R. B.

ISBN 978-1-338-60249-4

Text © 2019 by Kathryn Heling and Deborah Hembrook. Illustrations © 2019 by Rosie Butcher. All rights reserved. Published by Scholastic Inc., 557 Broadway, New York, NY 10012, by arrangement with Sterling Publishing Co., Inc. SCHOLASTIC and associated logos are trademarks and/or registered trademarks of Scholastic Inc.

The publisher does not have any control over and does not assume any responsibility for author or third-party websites or their content.

12 11 10   21 22 23 24

Printed in the U.S.A.   40

First Scholastic printing, September 2019

Book design by Ryan Thomann
The artwork for this book was created digitally.

There's Only One YOU

by **Kathryn Heling** and **Deborah Hembrook**
illustrated by **Rosie Butcher**

SCHOLASTIC INC.

In all the world over,
this much is true:

You're somebody special.
There's only one you.

Your knees might feel knobby;
your ears might stick out.
Are you tall? Are you short?
Are you thin? Are you stout?

You might be outgoing,
or maybe you're meek.
Whatever—it's awesome,
being unique!

Do your feelings spill out?

Do they lay low and hide?

You might cry when you're sad
or keep tears inside.

Do you smile just a bit
or laugh loud with a shriek?

You're different—it's awesome,
being unique!

Your color of skin is a beautiful sight,
light as the moon or dark as the night.

Your skin is so perfect,
from toes to your cheeks.
It's truly splendiferous
being unique!

Your hair might be curly
or a long, thick cascade,
worn short in a buzz cut
or tied in a braid.

RING-TAILED LEMUR
(LEMUR CATTA)

Your hair might be poofy,
or straight, smooth, and sleek.

PRIMATES

It's wild, it's wonderful
being unique!

TAPANULI ORANGUTAN
(PONGO TAPANULIENSIS)

When there's something to say,
do you talk with your hands?

Do you speak with an accent
from faraway lands?

Some voices are booming,

and some, just a squeak.

Your way is the best way
of being unique!

Can you sing? Do you dance?
Sports and drawing are fun.
Good at spelling or math?
Do you like more than one?

$2 + 2 = 4$
$2 + 4 = 6$
$2 + 6 = 8$

Is building for you?
Or gymnastic techniques?
It's great—celebrate
being unique!

You might have cool glasses
that help you to see.
A wheelchair or walker
gives mobility!

A hearing aid helps you to hear people speak.

Listen! It's glorious being unique!

Friends come in bunches
or groups of a few.
But maybe just one friend
is perfect for you.

Do you play with your friends
once a day? Once a week?
It's fun; it's fabulous,
being unique!

When it's time to dig in
and learn something new,
there's more than one way
of seeing it through.

You can work slow and steady
or in a fast streak.
Your brain grows in *your* way,
being unique!

Families are families,
but soon you will find

that each can be different—
a "best-for-them" kind.

You're part of a family.
You make it complete.

Hurrah for the one that's yours—
it's unique!

In all the world over,
this much is true:

You're special—unique.
There's just **one** of you!

Kathryn Heling and **Deborah Hembrook** are co-authors of over a dozen books for young children. Kathryn is a retired school psychologist who loves spending time with her grandchildren. She and her husband live in Madison, Wisconsin. Deborah teaches 4K, which she describes as "living her passion." She and her husband live in Germantown, Wisconsin.

Rosie Butcher lives in East Yorkshire, England, with her family. When she isn't drawing pictures, she spends time with her husband, Lee, and daughter, Penelope. They enjoy feeding birds, pointing out cobwebs, and building blanket forts on the sofa. Rosie's passions are painting, reading science books, and going on adventures.